I0602848

WINNING EMMA

SURRENDERED HEARTS - BOOK THREE

ROSIE CHAPEL

First printing 2018

ISBN: 978-0-6488365-2-0 (e-book)
ISBN: 978-0-6451116-7-5 (paperback)

Ulfire Pty. Ltd.
P.O. Box 1481
South Perth
WA 6951
Australia

www.rosiechapel.com

Cover designed by R Chapel

Cover Image: Courtesy Fairytale Design (Małgorzata Duvendack) with Deposit Photos

❀ Created with Vellum

ACKNOWLEDGMENTS

In gratitude to Jade Royal for inviting me to contribute to the anthology in which this was originally published. I appreciate your faith in me.

Heartfelt appreciation to Maria, Amy, Melanie, Jackie, and Brian for suffering my constant questions about covers and content.

Thank you to Graham from Fading Street Publishing Services, for his proofreading wizardry.

Winning Emma
Surrendered Hearts - Book 3

A Regency Novelette

Love is not a game, and there are no rules ~
in order to win, you must surrender

PROLOGUE

JUNE 1817

*E*mma Newbury leant on the frame of the huge, wooden, and at the moment open, front doors of Aspley Manor. Her gaze roamed over the lawns, to the slightly untamed flowerbeds. Their riotous profusion of colour almost painful to the eye on this bright summer's morning. Then, beyond to the scattering of oak and copper beech which stood like sentinels along the driveway.

She could hear people talking, but it was muted, and she surmised they were in her father's study at the far side of the entrance hall. She supposed they might like some refreshments, but she had no idea how to heat the water to make coffee or tea. *Pathetic*. Sighing, she straightened up and turned from the view, of which she never tired, into the cool dimness of the house.

Trailing into the study, she saw the four men surrounding Papa's desk. They were combing through papers, adding some to a neat stack of ledgers at one side, tossing others into the fire, their conversation conducted in undertones. Emma nearly laughed out loud. Since her father's death this house had been like a tomb, no one raised their voice, no one smiled. Yes, the circumstances were grim, but life had to go on, and she was beginning to wonder when, or whether, the pall would lift. It was too quiet, and of late, Emma often had to quash an irresistible urge to burst into song, or shout random words, or worse, whistle — a positively unseemly habit.

Her mother and younger sister, Sybil, had departed over a week ago, travelling to the Cotswolds, where they would take up residence with an elderly aunt and uncle. The staff left four days after that — new positions found for all of them. Fortunately for the tenant farmers, their livelihoods were secure as the estate required managing. Emma was the sole remaining occupant of Aspley Manor — but the house she had lived in since her birth was no longer her home.

The visitors glanced up at the sound of her footfall, which echoed in the unnatural silence.

"I am afraid I cannot offer you a hot beverage," a faint blush warmed her cheeks at having to admit their lack of domestic help, despite the fact these men already knew, "but I am sure there is some lemonade in the kitchens, or, if you prefer something stronger, we have wine and spirits."

"Thank you, my dear, a glass of whisky apiece would be appreciated." Henry Troughton, Duke of Driffield, smiled gently at the pale young woman hovering on the threshold, wishing, not for the first time, she would smile back.

He disliked being a party to this task, but it was essential, and he would rather it was he, than someone with no sympathy for the family. Not only had Charles, the late Viscount Aspley, been a distant relative — a cousin on his mother's side — he was also a friend.

The circumstances leading up to this point were murky, necessitating lengthy investigation, and the two men had agreed the only way to help Charles was for him to transfer the deeds for his properties to Henry, giving them some breathing space to uncover the truth. Regrettably, Charles' sudden death put an end to their objectives, although at least the manor was safe for the foreseeable future.

Now, Henry was trying to pick up the pieces with as little disruption as possible and had asked Emma to join his family at Driffield Park, as a companion, of sorts, to his own daughter, Charity. Long overindulged, Charity was in danger of becoming quite the obnoxious madam — her father at a loss as to how to deal with her wilful petulance, his patience hanging by a thread. He was hoping Emma's generally serene and sensible attitude might prove a stabilising influence.

In her turn, while she poured the drinks, Emma studied the newcomers covertly. Uncle Henry, as she had called his Grace since her childhood, was a regular guest at Aspley Manor, but the trio who accompanied him were strangers, and their presence sent an icy finger down her spine. Why were they here? What could Papa possibly have kept in his study that was of interest? No one thought to enlighten her, she was female, and therefore not privy to business dealings, but Emma was an astute young woman and all this secrecy frustrated her.

The three were tall and broad-shouldered, and all carried an aura of calm authority. Muscles flexed under fine wool coats when they lifted papers or stretched across the desk, their movements efficient, as though this was something they did frequently, and maybe they did — how would she know? All clean shaven, with contrasting shades of hair: raven, caramel, and deep auburn. *Really, Emma,* she chastised internally, *you sound like you've swallowed Chrétien de Troyes, romantic tarradiddle.* That did not stop her from wondering what colour their eyes were, and as she placed the drinks on the desk, they looked up to thank her.

Two had brown eyes, but he of the raven hair was the possessor of an unnervingly hypnotic grey-green gaze, which bore into her. She opened her mouth to say something, anything, but the words lodged in her throat when she scanned his angular features. *Dear lord, he was wickedly handsome. Did he have any idea of the power he could wield with a single glance?* Unable to tear her eyes away, she stared, a nameless sensation fluttering in her chest. Then she saw the corners of his mouth curve into a sardonic smile. Vexed at being caught ogling, Emma tilted her chin, her eyes flashing, the first sign of any animation since the men's arrival the previous day.

She dipped a neat curtsy. "My apologies. I wanted to commit the faces of those pawing through my father's life to memory. I hope you find what you seek, but I fail to see what purpose this achieves," she waved her hand towards the desk. "He is dead and buried; the reason for his actions died with him. What point is there in raking over what cannot be altered?" She felt the threat of tears and blinked furiously. Facing the duke, she added, "My luggage is packed, your Grace. The house, save this room, is closed up. I shall be on the terrace." Spinning on her heel, Emma fled before she made a complete fool of herself.

The four men stared at each other, maybe a trifle uncomfortably. In their haste to get what they needed, they had forgotten this was someone's home.

"She is not ordinarily so... temperamental," the duke offered, in a bid to excuse Emma's unusual behaviour.

"It is of no matter, doubtless she is overwrought," one of the men, Nathaniel Livingston, replied absently, engrossed in his task.

"Rather an unprepossessing young lady," the man with the sardonic smile interjected.

"Not very fair, Randi. She's probably not at her best at present. Everything she knows has just been tipped on its head," Nathaniel reproved. Randi shrugged and turned his attention back to the task at hand, effectively relegating Emma, and her temper to the far reaches of his mind.

Emma did not forget their intrusion into her life, but she could not have imagined just how insensitive fate could be.

CHAPTER 1

NOVEMBER 1819

"*M*arried? *Married*!" Randolph Craythorpe, Earl of Brackley, spat the words in fury. How the devil could she go from gentle flirting, and several dances an evening with him, to married? In the space of a fortnight no less. "Who is the lucky *gentleman?*" he gibed, his brain refusing to accept that Lady Felicity Hartwich, with whom he had shared more than one stolen kiss, and who seemed to return his affection, had upped and wed another, virtually under his nose.

"Timothy Archibald," Nathaniel Livingston, one of Randolph's two best friends replied.

"Westmoreland? That chinless wonder? Is this some kind of joke?" Timothy Archibald, the Duke of Westmoreland was a good fifteen years older than Randolph, and a man with little to attract a beautiful and much younger lady, except, of course, his wealth and his title.

"No joke, Randi. I believe it was an arrangement between him and the Hartwich family. Important enough that West-moreland applied for a special licence." Nathaniel watched his friend carefully. As a general rule, Randolph was easy going, and it took a lot to rile him up. Unfortunately, when something tipped him over the edge, he forgot he was the first son of a marquis and tended to get roaring drunk which inevitably led to his behaviour deteriorating into the pugnacious.

"I need a drink"

"You do not, 'tis barely midday. What you need is a diversion." Nathaniel tapped his lips contemplatively. His wife, Juliette, mentioned her cousin would be arriving soon, from Bath, to spend the Christmas season with them. Juliette was not a fan of said cousin, whom she considered selfish and conceited, but perhaps she might be the answer to an as yet unuttered prayer. "I have a suggestion." Randolph glared at him. "Hear me out." Going onto explain about the cousin.

"You want me to act as a babysitter for some silly debutante? That sounds like out of the frying pan and into the fire, Nate." Randolph was about to stomp off in high dudgeon when Nathaniel's next words gave him pause.

"It would make Lady Felicity jealous…" Nathaniel let that dangle, aware he was on thin ice. He had never met this cousin — she might have no looks of which to speak, but he was desperate enough to try anything. Randolph had never shown any interest in courtship until he met Felicity, and the two had appeared smitten with each other.

Nathaniel frowned, in all honesty, he did not like Lady Felicity. She seemed… what was the word… detached, aloof maybe. In his opinion, not good enough for his friend, although he would never admit this to Randolph. There were no rules when it came to love, those who claimed your heart often proved to be the most unsuitable — a hint of a smile tugging on his lips when he thought of Juliette. What there *were* rules for was Society, and right now Nathaniel needed Randolph to appear unmoved by the news that the woman he had fallen for had just married someone else.

. . .

About to reject Nate's proposal, Randolph heard the word 'jealous'. His lip curled in the parody of a grin and he found himself agreeing. If Felicity could treat him in so cavalier a manner, he was quite capable of returning the favour.

"Fine, but I reserve the right to renege on this agreement should she prove less homely than a church mouse."

Nathaniel hid a triumphant grin. Schooling his features, he inclined his head in grave acknowledgement, then invited Randolph to join Juliette and him for dinner that evening. It was easier to keep an eye on him that way!

Despite the best intentions of his friends, ten days and an outsize in headaches later, Randolph was still wallowing in self-pity. Juliette was no longer certain she wanted her cousin within a mile of the earl, his behaviour too immoderate even to be wished on so detested a relative.

The evening before the anticipated arrival of the guests, Nathaniel and Ged Mowbray, the third member of their group, took Randolph aside in the hopes of impressing upon him that being sober when introduced to Lady Charity was of paramount importance.

"Look at you," Ged scolded. "You look like a profligate rake and stink like a brothel. Why the major continues to trust you is beyond me." Referring to Major Withers, the man to whom all three were answerable.

"Because he knows I am the best." Randolph slurred, pointing a finger at his chest, his eyes bloodshot and bleary. Nathaniel and Ged looked at each other, then back to Randolph.

"No help for it," Nathaniel remarked, meditatively.

"Only way," Ged agreed.

Each hooking an arm through one of Randolph's, they dragged him backwards down the slight slope to the bottom of the Livingston's garden.

"Sorry, Randi," Neither sounded particularly apologetic, and giving Randolph no chance to protest, dumped him bodily into the small pond. He landed with a loud splash, and for a few seconds was submerged completely. There was a subdued roar when he reared up, shaking his head, water spraying everywhere. Saturated from head to foot, and in a towering rage, Randolph stood in the middle of the pond, which was only knee deep, and glared at his friends, so angry, words failed him.

"You reckon that did the trick?" Ged asked, studying his sodden friend dispassionately.

"Hope so, the fish couldn't take another dunking," Nathaniel replied with a chuckle, as the two turned their backs and strolled up to the house. Juliette met them on the terrace, arms folded, foot tapping,

"What did you do?"

"Randi will likely need to borrow some of my clothes." Nathaniel adroitly sidestepped his wife's question.

"Ged?" She pinned her gaze on his friend. Ged shrugged and raised his hands, palms up.

"He had it coming."

"'Tis the middle of winter, he'll catch his death. I am surprised the pond wasn't frozen."

"It might have been, but let's just say Randi was offering a service to the birds. They needed a drink."

"Oh, you…" Juliette's exasperation was easily mollified when Nathaniel dropped a kiss on her forehead.

"I apologise he has suffered a soaking, my love, but he needs to pull himself together. Charity arrives tomorrow, and if he has any chance of persuading Felicity her marriage has not affected him, he needs to have his head in the game, not buried in a vat of whisky."

While they were talking, another lady joined them. Tall, with a swathe of jet-black hair artfully styled over her face, Melissa Bouchard was Ged's very new betrothed. A state of affairs that shocked Society, as neither were considered marriageable. Born with a twisted foot, and her lovely complexion marred by a purple birthmark which ran from the lobe of her right ear, across the edge of her cheek and halfway down her neck, Melissa had long believed she would never marry, for who would see past her flaws? Gerard Mowbray simply did not see why he should be saddled with a wife when he could satisfy his urges without any commitment at all. Recently, Melissa had proposed an intriguing wager, which seemed the answer to their prayers, but somewhere along the way, they realised the last thing either of them wanted had become their dearest wish.

"Randi always keeps things close to his chest. He appears to float through life without a care, absolutely unflappable. This business with Felicity has jerked him out of his customary complaisance. I have never seen him so ill-tempered." Melissa's thoughtful interjection prompted nods all round.

"We'll get him through this. He just needs to sober up. I thought I could hold my liquor, Randi could beat me into a cocked hat." Ged took Melissa's hand and drew her close. "Trust us."

"I always do," she murmured, resting her head against his shoulder for a heartbeat, before becoming her usual, practical self. "No time to dawdle. Come, Juliette, let us see whether our esteemed Lord Brackley might appreciate a towel and a hot drink. Mayhap our feminine concern will soothe his wrath."

Trying not to chortle at the bedraggled mess that was currently Randolph Craythorpe, Melissa made her way towards the pond, to offer what assistance she could, while Juliette rang for a maid to fetch a towel and lay out a set of fresh clothing in one of the guest rooms. Thankfully, Randolph and Nathaniel were of similar build and once the former was dressed, they persuaded him to drink nothing stronger than hot chocolate for the rest of the evening.

CHAPTER 2

*T*he entourage bearing Lady Charity Anscombe was delayed by a day. The weather had deteriorated, and heavy snow hampered travellers heading into London from whichever direction. Thus, it was a fatigued and rather crotchety group who arrived late one snowy Saturday afternoon, three weeks before Christmas.

Hearing the commotion, Juliette and Nathaniel made their way to the entrance hall, smiles at the ready.

An imperious voice floated through the front door. "Do be careful with my luggage. Honestly, you would think my cousin could afford decent staff, it is London after all."

Juliette grimaced and looked at her husband. Nathaniel, who had suggested Charity would find Radclyffe House — Juliette's parents' home and a far more opulent abode — more suited to her taste, was clenching his teeth, and the woman had not yet made it through their door.

"Patience, Nate. Let us assume she is merely fractious because of the arduous journey. I shall apologise to our staff later. Please do not make this any more difficult by being angry, however righteously."

Nathaniel huffed a sigh and forced a smile. "Fret not, my love, I shall be the consummate host. Although, I may find I have many, *many* tasks to which I absolutely must attend." Winking, he gave Juliette a quick hug and suffered an elbow to his side.

"'Tis a good job I love you."

Any further conversation was curtailed when Lady Charity sailed into the house. Juliette had not seen her cousin for at least a decade, but she would recognise her anywhere. Diminutive in stature, Charity was undeniably beautiful, but her blonde hair, vivid blue eyes, flawless complexion, and impeccable deportment, concealed a domineering and wholly autocratic personality. She could turn on the charm when necessary, but pity the poor soul who thwarted her, however inadvertently.

Once on the receiving end of her displeasure, you were forever thereafter *persona non grata*. In the main, this was the reason for Juliette's astonishment when she received Charity's letter a month previously, begging to stay with her. The cousins had never been close — in fact, they barely tolerated each other. Juliette was not known for her tact, and Charity rubbed her up the wrong way with her supercilious behaviour. It was conceivable she had increased in her cousin's estimation by marrying Nathaniel. For although being the fourth son, he had no chance at the marquisate, his family's status was higher than that of the St Clairs... Juliette's father — a mere earl. Moreover, as Charity never did anything spontaneously, Juliette assumed there was an ulterior motive, not yet disclosed.

Ignoring her misgivings, Juliette swept forward and took control, greeting her cousin and her accompanying staff, while tacitly thanking her foresight in preparing all the bedchambers.

"Charity, my dear, welcome to Northcote House, how wonderful to see you. I hope the delays have not proven too irksome. Jane will see you to your bedchamber, where you might like to freshen up. We have guests joining us for dinner who are on tenterhooks to meet you and hear all about the social whirl of Bath."

"Oh, Bath… so refined. Far more beneficial to those with a delicate constitution, such as I." Charity waved her hand languidly, as she bussed the air near Juliette's cheek. Juliette swallowed a grin. Charity had the constitution of an ox but managed to appear fragile, as though a puff of wind would blow her away. Deliberately pushing that very tempting thought aside, she escorted Charity up the stairs. Halfway up, Juliette threw a speaking glance over her shoulder at Nathaniel, who nodded his understanding and corralled the remainder of the new arrivals. Soon, people and luggage were dispatched to whichever corner of the house they belonged, and the hall fell quiet.

Presuming everyone was accounted for, Nathaniel went to close the front door before heading to the drawing room, where he believed a snifter of whisky awaited. He was surprised to see a tall woman, in a drab grey travelling outfit, the brim of her hat low over her face, trudging up the steps, with… wait… was that a *dog*?

"Forgive me…" not sure who this person was, he went with "…my lady. I thought everyone was already inside."

"Please do not concern yourself. Charity asked that I take charge of Bertie, and he needed to relieve himself after being restrained in the carriage." Smiling wearily, she closed the front door and leant against it as though gathering her strength. "I do apologise for Bertie, Charity refuses to leave him at home, but I daresay she forgot to ask whether you minded her bringing him. He is a well-behaved little creature generally, and rarely barks. I have his things here." She lifted the large carpet bag she was holding. "If you and your wife have no objections to his staying in Charity's bedchamber, might you be so kind as to direct me there, so I may reunite them?"

This was delivered in colourless tones that matched her gown, perplexing Nathaniel, who rang for a maid. Who on earth was this self-possessed young woman and how did she fit into the picture? She seemed vaguely familiar, but he had never been to Bath, so could not see how their paths might have crossed. As though reading his mind she added, just as Jane came down the stairs.

"Where are my manners. Good afternoon, my lord. I am Emma Newbury, Lady Charity's… companion." A word so laden with abhorrence, Nathaniel blinked, at the same time as the name rang a distant bell. The woman's expression had not changed and for a split second, he thought he had imagined it. He needed to talk to Juliette, she would know. For now, he bowed and said he looked forward to seeing her at dinner.

Emma groaned to herself. How on earth was she supposed to endure this? She was in the home of one of the three men who had accompanied Uncle Henry to Aspley Manor, who had rifled through her father's desk, who had violated his privacy when he was scarcely cold in his grave. The day she left everything she had ever known. Of all the rotten luck. She made a mental note to be as unobtrusive as possible; hopefully he would not recall her outburst or recognise her name.

The evening was not as fraught as it might have been. Dinner guests arrived and, after introductions were made and an aperitif enjoyed, they all moved to the dining room where a simple but delicious repast was served.

Charity did see fit to complain about everything, but Juliette smoothed it over as did, to everyone else's surprise, Randolph. He had not touched spirits for two days and, following his unceremonious drenching, took a long hard look at himself, concluding he was a thoroughly pathetic excuse of a human being. Consequently, he decided to make an extra effort and went out of his way to assuage Charity's grievances. By the end of the meal, she had lost her discontented look and was becoming quite the chatterbox, vacuous though her topics of conversation seemed to be.

In vain, Juliette and Melissa tried to steer the discussion away from hurtful gossip, but Charity seemed to delight in it; the more malicious, the happier she was. Juliette recalled all the reasons she avoided the yearly summons to Driffield Park, using her younger sister Letitia — four years her junior and, until recently, considered far too young for so adult a gathering, as an excuse. If Juliette remained at home to chaperone Letitia, her mother would feel more inclined to go — an arrangement, which benefitted everyone. She dragged her mind back to the conversation in time to hear Charity say.

"Of course, being as generous as my parents has its drawbacks. There is the common assumption one's coffers are bottomless, or our doors are open to every family member fallen on hard times, however distant, as poor Emma knows all too well. If her imbecile of a father had not behaved in so reprehensible a manner, I would not be stuck with a companion more interested in books than balls."

CHAPTER 3

*T*here was a stunned silence. As though drawn by magnets, all eyes swivelled to Emma who looked serenely indifferent. The niggling suspicion he knew her continued to nudge at Nathaniel's subconscious, but refused to be pinned down. The same sentiment swept over Ged and Randolph, but neither were any the wiser than Nathaniel.

"Charity," Juliette hissed in outraged undertones, "do behave yourself. Emma is a guest in my home and shall be treated with the same respect as any other."

"Oh, Emma does not mind, do you?" Charity said flippantly, a languid hand waving in Emma's general direction.

"Maybe not, but I do," Nathanial interjected quietly. "I applaud anyone who has the courage to follow a path previously unchartered, whether by choice or circumstance. There by the grace of God." Biting down on a bark of mirth when he saw Charity's mouth drop open in unladylike astonishment. Before he said anything he might regret, he stood and invited Ged and Randolph to join him in the drawing room for cigars — more to put a distance between himself and Charity, than anything else.

. . .

At the same time, Emma asked to be excused, pleading Bertie's evening walk as the reason, which did not fool anyone. She bobbed a curtsy and left the room, head held high, cursing her flaming cheeks. Charity's lack of tact was bad enough, what made it worse was that she had belittled her in front of all three men from that awful day, although, to be scrupulously fair, Charity could not have known.

Despite it being over two years ago, when Lord Brackley was introduced, it might as well have been yesterday, and that same nameless sensation rippled through her. She was thankful to note he did not seem to remember her.

Once in the cool of the garden, watching Bertie snuffling through the snow, her mortification subsided. She should be accustomed to it by now. Charity never missed an opportunity to draw attention to Emma's father's *mistake*.

Emma frowned, was the death of Viscount Aspley, just as he was to hand over the estate to Uncle Henry — better known as the Duke of Driffield and Charity's father, more than just coincidence? When the sordid details were revealed, Emma was unable to equate the man, the caring, loving father she knew, with the person who had gambled away the family fortunes and tried to cover the losses through shady business dealings. It staggered her that he had managed to keep his financial straits from the rest of his family. His only recourse — to surrender his inheritance.

In less than three days, they went from a life untroubled to one they scarcely recognised. Emma lost her home, what was left of her family and, given no real alternative, acceded to Uncle Henry's wishes, becoming companion to his irresponsible daughter. It had been the duke's heartfelt wish that Emma's tranquil presence would curb his daughter's wild, thoughtless, sometimes cruel ways, and, in turn, Charity might realise not all genteel pursuits were boring and useless. Sadly, this was not the case. Charity had no desire to become an unattractive and uninteresting wallflower, which was how she viewed and constantly described Emma, and Emma had long given up caring.

To give him his due, the duke was never anything other than kind to Emma, almost apologetic that he had no alternative but to seize Newbury lands and oust her family. The duchess was another story; a less spiteful version of Charity, who, nonetheless, delighted in lording it over their newly impecunious relation. Emma was moved to wonder why Uncle Henry married her — a vapid individual with all the personality of a chair, but reasoned it was probably arranged, likely before his birth. Charity was their only child, for which Emma hoped the world would be grateful, but so domineering was she that oft it seemed there were three of her.

Emma had forgotten what it was like to feel happy and carefree.

The last two years had been… a challenge. Like the rest of the *ton*, Emma never expected the *status quo* to change, but it did, and she had gained an abiding appreciation for people less fortunate, especially those in service. Emma was once a vivacious young lady, but Charity's perpetual demands and snide remarks had undermined her self-confidence and she was a subdued version of her former self. Her future looked bleak, there was no prospect of marriage, let alone a good one, and once Charity decided she could no longer stomach a companion, Emma expected to be asked to leave Driffield Park — something she both desired and feared.

Bertie whined, breaking into her reverie. Huffing a resigned sigh, she picked him up, burying her face in his soft fur, his canine affection provoking an absurd desire to weep. Refusing to succumb to such nonsense, Emma swallowed hard, carried the little dog into the warmth of the house and upstairs to Charity's bedchamber.

She did not rejoin the gathering.

Leaning against the mantelpiece in the drawing room, Randolph spied a figure strolling aimlessly in the snow blanketed garden. Puzzled that anyone would be abroad in such weather, he wandered to the window. It was Miss Newbury. Something about this woman intrigued him, the peculiar flicker of recognition he felt in the dining room returned to pester him. Wearing a grey cloak, its hood covering her dark brown hair, which he recalled had been scraped back into a tidy bun, she seemed to blend into the shadows. Very tall, with a figure that, despite her effort to disguise it under drab attire, could only be described as voluptuous... *voluptuous... dash it all Randi where did **that** come from?* He had no interest in Miss Emma Newbury, she was not his type at all; plain, too... hmm... curvy was the politest term, and lacking any of the attributes he found attractive. He much preferred petite blondes — just like Charity, in fact, and was irritated when he found himself trying to recall the colour of Emma's eyes.

He watched as she picked up the little dog, pausing for a long moment, her face hidden in the creature's fur. His brow creased, and he felt an unaccountable tightening in his chest when she deliberately straightened her shoulders and headed away from the garden towards the back door. Trying to discern what prompted it, he realised it was because she seemed unutterably lonely.

It was an image which refused to be banished.

As the days unfolded, Randolph and Emma seldom met. Emma continued to cling to the periphery of every gathering she had no alternative but to attend, and Randolph, although unable to shake the notion he knew Emma, had what he considered to be far more important things on his mind.

Emma could not remain completely invisible, neither could she ignore the people around her, and had no mind to appear impolite to her hosts. One thing she had always relished was lively debate, something her father had encouraged, and which occurred with gratifying frequency at Northcote House. Juliette and Nathaniel eschewed the *ton's* preference for mind-numbing chit-chat about trivial matters when dining, preferring to discuss politics or the latest social and economic issues. Initially, Emma was reserved, it was not her place to comment, but the Livingstons and their friends drew her into their discourse. Before many days passed, she had become quite comfortable offering her opinion or arguing a point, much to Charity's indignation.

Randolph was intrigued by Emma's obvious intelligence, wit, and lack of artifice, and for reasons he could not fathom, sought her out for an occasional conversation. Nothing serious, but he appreciated her viewpoint, and discovered her to be a sympathetic listener when he had cause to vent his spleen. Oddly, the rather forlorn image of Emma standing in the snow continued to haunt Randolph, and Emma found, to her chagrin that Randolph had taken up residence in her dreams.

Both found it quite mystifying.

CHAPTER 4

One morning maybe a week after arriving in London, Emma was curled up on the window seat in the library, buried in a book, concealed behind the heavy curtain. She savoured these brief periods when she had no chores to complete or messages to take. So absorbed was she, it took several seconds to register she was not alone. About to fling back the curtain to apprise whoever it was of her presence, her hand was stayed when she heard mention of her name.

"If you no longer require her, why not ask your father to release her?" It was Lord Brackley, Randolph.

"Papa likes her," Charity's sulky voice replied. Emma closed her eyes, her stomach plummeting. Whatever they were about to say did not bode well. Moreover, she knew the adage about those who eavesdrop.

"Surely once you reach your majority, his Grace cannot force you to retain her as your companion?"

A weighty sigh. "Papa thinks she is a steadying influence, and because she likes books and learning, it will rub off on me." A crow of derisive laughter. "Honestly, she is the dreariest person I know; boring, plain, and dull. If I ever have trouble falling asleep, I think of Emma, the soporific effect is immediate."

A curious silence, then, "She might be plain, but I did not think her dull, and books can be quite stimulating."

"Not you as well? Mayhap I should find another beau to escort me to these insufferable balls."

An amused chuckle. "Come now, my lady, after all we have achieved, you do not mean that."

"Give me ten minutes and I shall be ready." Footsteps and the door swung closed.

Emma strove to quell angry tears. She hated being beholden, it was the worst feeling in the world. She had a mind to leave, pack her meagre belongings, thank her hosts, and just go, disappear into the big wide world, where no one knew her. She probably had enough coin to get her out of London. Maybe she could find employment in one of the country estates. Even as this ran through her head, she knew it was futile. *How could she get work? She had no references. Maybe a shop would hire her…?*

Dropping the book on the ledge, she pushed back the curtain and took two steps in the room.

Randolph was still there.

Hang it all!

An odd sound had Randolph spinning around — his eyes falling on Emma, her pallor indicating she had heard his exchange with Charity.

"Miss Newbury, I beg your pardon. I thought we were alone."

"Which of course makes it acceptable to disparage the help." The last word practically a sneer.

"No, of course not... I... 'tis just..." Randolph clamped his mouth closed. There was nothing he could say.

Her face was devoid of expression. "Do not give it a thought, my lord. After all, I am just a servant," she flipped a hand when Randolph tried to repudiate it, "by any other name... companion is only used so as not to offend Lady Charity's..." she paused, and Randolph thought he discerned a flicker of emotion, an underlying distress, quickly masked, "...sensitivities. I do not expect you to have any concept of what it is like to be at someone else's beck and call, day and night. To pander to every whim without a word of complaint, to be made to feel your worth is somewhere beneath that of the scullery maid, and your presence is suffered because others laud the generosity of those who took you in. They are your benefactor; no hint of censure may be uttered against them. It is a state of affairs which would be harsh enough if you were born into the servant class, it is far worse when once you lived in the lap of luxury, cosseted and pampered! Then, in an instant, it is stripped away, and you are left to beg for whatever scraps are thrown from the lofty tables of Society. I hope you appreciate what you have — to take it for granted is a grave mistake."

Emma bent her head, trying to collect her thoughts, she knew her words were inexcusable, but could not stop them spilling over. Too long had she held everything inside, too long had she closed her mind to the humiliation she had no alternative but to endure. It did not help that this man had seen her, had witnessed her family's fall from grace, had hunted through her father's papers, through his desk, scrutinising every facet of his life, and had not the courtesy to recall any of it. Then, to add insult to injury, Emma knew the growing sentiment she continued to deny was not only futile, it would also remain unrequited, for even had he not been enamoured of Charity, she was beneath his notice.

How galling.

She raised her eyes to his, and Randolph flinched at the desolation in her gaze. "I was like you once — never hesitating to fling out an order, never noticing those who carried it out, often forgetting to thank them. Now, I am neither maid nor mistress, my status is nebulous. I have to be acknowledged, I am Lady Charity's companion, but I am also an embarrassment to her, to them. Nevertheless, I do thank you for saying books can be stimulating, at least we agree on that." Pale, and trembling with suppressed emotion, Emma dipped an excuse of a curtsey, lifted her chin, and hurried out.

Randolph was frozen in place. Her words cut him to the quick. Was he really so callous? He ran his mind over the last few years. No, he was not callous. Indifferent maybe, occasionally tactless, and yes, he could be insensitive, but definitely not callous. At least he had not been until Felicity's heartless conduct. Could he blame her? No, although Felicity was not faultless — her behaviour precipitated this, he was the one who chose to act like a boor. It did not help that Emma's face still pulled at the back of his mind, while her identity remained tantalisingly out of reach. He would have to ask Nate.

He heard the thud of footsteps on the stairs and schooled his expression. Seconds later Charity blew into the library wrapped up in an expensive winter cloak, fur lining the hood. She looked like a fairy princess, but another face — pale, irate and definitely *not* plain — dominated his thoughts.

Temperatures plummeted, the snow hardened, and frost coated the landscape, transforming London into a sparkling winter wonderland of silver, grey and white, alleviated here and there by dark boughs of evergreen — holly, pine, and yew.

Charity declared she had no intention of venturing out for anything other than a visit to her modiste or whatever ball to which she had finagled an invitation. She did not, however, have any compunction dispatching Emma on all manner of errands, from buying ribbons to leaving calling cards at the homes of her friends across the city, for surely, they would be overjoyed to know she had arrived.

Randolph played his part with aplomb. Charity's volatile behaviour washed over him like waves ebbing from a beach. He seemed unaffected or unaware of her sharp tongue and haughty demands, indulging her every request.

His two friends and their wives were floored. None wanted to be in the young woman's presence any more than necessary. Even Juliette, who rued the day she responded to Charity's not so subtle entreaty that she be invited to London for Christmas, struggled to maintain her polite façade, and Charity was her cousin — yet Randolph actively sought her out. He had already escorted her to three soirees and two balls and indicated he would continue in the same vein.

Although this was the plan, to prove to Felicity that Randolph was unmoved by her betrayal, none expected him to be quite so... enthusiastic. Juliette was concerned enough to ask Nathaniel to intervene. Charity would eat Randolph for breakfast if he went and fell in love with her — and he did not deserve that.

Of what no one else was cognisant, was neither Randolph nor Charity bore one crumb of sentimental affection for the other. Each was playing a part. Randolph's was already known, but Charity had her eye on Lord Spencer Fitzroy, son of the Duke of Newborough, whom she met in Bath at the end of the Season. He had been very attentive, but rumours were circulating that his eye was wandering. Charity was not about to let some flighty debutante steal him out from under her nose, and Randolph, who contrary to current opinion was *not* blind to Charity's faults, sympathised — his own experience not far removed.

The pair discussed their strategy with a ruthless reasoning more akin to a military campaign than a romantic interlude. Charity found it highly entertaining to aid and abet Randolph's cause, and Randolph was more than happy to assist Charity in her endeavours. Lord Spencer would submit to her will in so subtle a manner, he would believe she was the one who had capitulated.

CHAPTER 5

*F*or her part, Emma had few complaints. Being at Charity's beck and call was a double-edged sword. If she tarried, she would likely receive a tongue lashing, but… if she was canny, she could *extend* any one of the tasks Charity sent her to fulfil.

Using the atrocious weather to her advantage, Emma claimed her errands were taking longer than anticipated, grasping every opportunity to discover bookshops, and art galleries, museums, and parks. Bertie also provided an excellent reason for leaving the confines of Northcote House; he needed two walks a day and Emma had no mind to deprive him of them.

It was her first visit to London, and the enormity of the city fascinated her. Having lived all her life on a country estate, the snow was no hindrance and, whenever possible, she vanished for hours.

No one thought to question Emma's absence or ask whether she might appreciate some company. She was, after all, part of that curiously unseen strata of society — the general factotum — not quite relegated to the domestic sphere but, undoubtedly due to regrettable circumstances, no longer considered part of the elite. Rarely seen, never heard, and oft ignored.

Thus, she always went alone. Solitude did not worry Emma, she treasured the luxury of silence. Until her father died, she would escape with a book and go down to the lake, or tuck in behind one of the curtained alcoves, quickly losing herself in worlds far beyond her home.

In the period following her father's death, the anomalous hush of Aspley Manor bothered her, and for a time she longed for the normal hubbub of a busy household. This changed once she was swallowed into Driffield Park, where she was lucky to snatch a moment of peace during the day. Here, she began to relish it once again.

These unanticipated free hours gave her plenty of time with her thoughts, and she began to ruminate on her father's disgrace. She wished she had been smart enough to go through his papers before Uncle Henry took possession of Aspley Manor. She supposed they had been destroyed, but what if that was not the case? What if there was information therein to prove her father's innocence? What if he had been coerced into confessing to something he had not done, for reasons never disclosed? In her heart of hearts, Emma knew she was clutching at straws, but she wanted to know the truth, even if that only confirmed the accusations were justified. She needed answers but had no coin to pay anyone to investigate.

Out of the blue, she recalled a comment Charity made when the Driffields received an invitation to Juliette's wedding. An event they declined to attend, because the hand-written card bearing the glad tidings indicated it would be an informal occasion, akin to a garden party, *oh goodness no* too, too provincial. Charity had rather disparagingly, remarked it was typical of Juliette to fall in love with a reprobate highwayman who, it transpired, was in the employ of the government.

Perhaps Juliette, or rather her husband, could help.

The following evening, Emma got her chance. Randolph had taken Charity to a musical gathering at the home of one the latter's acquaintances, so it was just the three of them. During dinner, Emma waited until there was an appropriate break in conversation and, sending up a soundless prayer, asked whether she might speak.

"Of course, Emma, you are as much a guest here as Charity. Please do not feel you have no voice. You are as welcome to chat as anyone." As she said this, Juliette's mind flew back over the week, horrified to realise this composed young woman, who was staying in her home had been largely ignored by everyone in the household. "Oh, Emma my dear, forgive me, I have been an appalling hostess. I am becoming one of those insensitive ladies I swore I would never be, careless and neglectful."

Emma sought to allay Juliette's consternation. "My lady, you have been kindness itself and certainly not insensitive. I admit I prefer to stay in the background, so 'tis easy to forget I am here. The reason for my question, is that I have a conundrum, which I need help solving." She paused. "I am not certain how much, if anything, Charity has told you of my… past," searching Juliette's face. Juliette looked blank. Encouraged, Emma forged ahead. "I was not always in service, but my family…" she tried to think of a less stark way of phrasing what had happened, choosing, "…fell on hard times and I was offered the position of companion to Charity, who is a relative of sorts." Feeling as though she should elaborate, she added, "My father was Viscount Aspley.

Juliette looked perplexed, but out of the corner of her eye, Emma knew she was not imagining the dawning comprehension on Nathaniel's face, as though he had just found the missing piece in a rather tricky puzzle. "My lord?" she ventured.

"Firstly, please call us by our given names, Miss Newbury, and secondly, am I correct in assuming we have met before?"

Emma nodded slowly, biting down on a wild giggle when Juliette glared at her husband, words tumbling from her mouth.

"Nathaniel Livingston, do you mean to tell me you know Emma, and somehow, despite the numerous times we are together throughout the day, did not feel it pertinent to apprise me of this fact? Never mind that this means Emma and I are related, however distantly, through Charity." Her voice rose dangerously.

"Juliette Livingston, while I admit something about Miss Newbury tweaked at my mind, I could not for the life of me remember why. It was hearing her father's title just now, which brought it all back." He leant back in his chair and opened his palms. "I cannot imagine what you went through that day and have borne since. Does your question perchance relate to whether your father was guilty as charged?"

"Yes," her voice little more than a whisper.

"The case is ongoing. However, on the proviso this stays

between us, I believe I can assure you Lord Aspley was not guilty of fraudulent practices, only of being too trusting and maybe a little gullible."

"He was innocent?" Emma squeaked in shock.

"While I am not at liberty to comment further, our inquiries uncovered an individual who, with his... errr... cronies, spun a web of lies, which trapped more than your father. It appears Lord Aspley did like to gamble, but he was not reckless, certainly not to the extent he would lose everything, and although his name was attributed to questionable business deals, it transpires his moniker and seal had been forged. Unfortunately, his premature death rather stymied our investigations. You may not be aware, but the Duke of Driffield and your father agreed to the transfer of property deeds, to give them time to uncover the perpetrator. The papers we collected that day gave us a few hints, but it has been a long road."

"What about the Manor?" Emma ventured.

"I cannot comment, but perhaps his Grace is the best person to talk with," Nathaniel replied, his tones sympathetic.

"It would be splendid if Mama and Sybil were able to return home and, hopefully, if Papa is absolved, Sybil might enjoy at least one Season."

"What about you?" Juliette interjected.

Emma shrugged. "What about me? My path is laid out. I might find work as a governess or companion to someone else, once Charity...errr... no longer requires me."

"Emma, you are the daughter of a viscount. Your place is in Society." Juliette countered, in consternation.

Emma laughed, but it was a humourless sound. "Yes, one who was disgraced and, regardless of whether he is exonerated, the majority will continue to believe he was not entirely innocent. By the time Sybil is old enough, I daresay the scandal will have been forgotten, but 'tis still too recent for me. I may be lucky enough to find a gentleman who can see beyond the rumours, but he will not be from the class I was born into. That said, I do confess to being inordinately delighted we are distantly related." She concluded, ingenuously.

While Emma's words sounded fatalistic, neither Juliette nor Nathaniel could refute them. Society was an unforgiving mistress and to be accepted back into the fold could be a formidable task.

"I shall keep you informed," Nathaniel said, then changed the subject. The remainder of the evening passed in light conversation, the three sharing snippets about their families over another glass, or two, of wine.

CHAPTER 6

The following morning, the snow had eased and, although bitterly cold, the sun was shining. Emma was looking forward to her usual walk with Bertie; an hour out of doors would be invigorating. It was far too early to tell Charity — that young woman would not rise before noon, having come home in the wee small hours — but politeness dictated she acquaint Juliette, who was busy writing letters, of her intention.

"I would love to come with you, but I must deal with this correspondence. I am woeful at keeping up to date with it." She smiled impishly, tugging a responding grin from Emma. "Which reminds me. We have been invited to a ball two evenings hence, and you shall come with us. No..." when Emma began to splutter a denial. "...'tis time you re-entered Society, if for no other reason than it lays the foundations for Sybil."

Juliette knew it was unfair using Emma's sister as incentive, but reasoned it was probably the only way she could persuade Emma to join them. Juliette was appalled by the misfortune which all but destroyed the Newbury family, leaving them destitute and reliant on the generosity of others — although generous was not a term she would use to describe Charity's attitude towards Emma.

She had lain awake the previous night, trying to come up with a plan to reintroduce Emma to the *ton*, and this seemed the ideal opportunity. Mindful that fans would be whispered behind, and disparaging comments would abound, Juliette was also of the belief it was better to face those who might judge, than remain in hiding.

Moreover, this way, Emma would not have to brave them on her own, she had support from within Society, and the fathers of Nathaniel, Ged, and Randolph were highly respected. Few would wish to come to their attention because they maligned a guest staying with one of their family or friends.

Emma desperately tried to extricate herself. "My lad… Juliette, thank you for so kind a gesture, but I have naught to wear, nor the wherewithal to purchase a gown suitable for the occasion. My appearance alongside you would only cause embarrassment."

"Tsk, what rubbish!" was Juliette's considered response. "We can procure a gown and shoes within the day at no cost to you, this is my treat. We shall visit my modiste this afternoon. Oh, what fun."

Once more, Emma attempted to stem Juliette's enthusiasm, to no avail. Finally, she acquiesced, with as much grace as possible, and affirmed she would return within the hour, escaping with Bertie into the chill morning.

Emma strolled to the nearby park, where she let Bertie chase about, expending his pent-up energy, while she attempted to wade through the tumult clouding her brain. An hour later, her head was no clearer, but she did feel refreshed. Juliette and she partook of a light luncheon, after which, the pair climbed into a carriage to be trundled into the heart of the city.

It was years since Emma had visited such an establishment, and then it was to one in Bath, which was sadly lacking in its… variety. Here in London, there was plenty of competition to clothe the *ton*, and she had never seen anything like Madame Renaud's. The choice of materials, of colours, of ribbons and buttons, of underclothes and shoes — not to mention all the essential accessories — was astonishing. Emma was exhausted before they started. Juliette, despite caring little about her own wardrobe, did love to dress other people, and often accompanied her younger sister to the dressmaker.

"Lady Juliette, how wonderful to see you, and who is your lovely companion?" Madame Renaud herself welcomed them, bustling the two women through to a large room at one side of the elegant reception area. Several chairs and a chaise were placed around the room and in the centre stood a large square box.

"Good afternoon, Madame. This is my friend, Miss Emma Newbury, who is in need of four new gowns and all the accoutrements. Hush…" when Emma made to interrupt, "…please, permit me this indulgence." Juliette held Emma's frantic gaze calmly.

"Thank you," Emma whispered, fighting an unexpected urge to cry. *Goodness, for someone who had not shed a tear since the death of her father, she was becoming a veritable watering pot.* Since arriving at the Livingstons, even before their conversation the previous night, Emma had been made very welcome and the kindness shown, touched her heart. The staff was warmly friendly, as were her hosts, even Ged, and Melissa.

Charity would never be cordial — Emma's presence was an irritation to be tolerated. To Emma's bewilderment, Randolph, their sporadic discussions aside, also treated her with reserve whenever they met which, to Emma's relief, was infrequently. As far as she could tell, Randolph had no recollection of the first time she was inexcusably rude, making his demeanour baffling. One minute he was cordial, the next reticent. His behaviour rankled, but the inexplicable ache in her chest it caused, puzzled her more.

Dragging her mind back, she concentrated on the utter joy of being pampered. Madame Renaud, loosed Emma's hair, letting the rich brown curls spill down her back, then told her to strip out of her day dress and stand on the box. Standing in front of Emma, Madame tilted her head back and forth, while an assistant took measurements.

"You are very tall, and your 'air is beautiful. I think... hmmm..." the modiste barked instructions, as minions scurried about bringing all manner of things — swatches of material, samples of ribbon. Madame held up each piece, either shaking or nodding her head.

What followed was an experience somewhere between exhilarating and terrifying, during which Emma was allowed no opinion.

"Tsk, tsk, Miss Newbury. Are you the modiste? Non, 'tis I, Madame Renaud. You are merely my momentary muse allowing me to display my expertise. Would you interfere with an artiste while 'e paints, or a... hmmm... musician while 'e plays? Non! Now..." she wandered off to the adjoining room, her French accent becoming more pronounced in her exasperation.

. . .

Emma glanced at Juliette who rolled her eyes. The gesture made Emma giggle, diffusing the tension and, all of a sudden, she relaxed. The rest of the afternoon sped by and when the two returned to Northcote House, they were chattering as though friends for years, not a matter of two weeks. Once inside, they parted ways, Juliette wanted to speak to cook, and Emma said she ought to see whether Charity required anything.

Still smiling, Emma peeked into the parlour and the drawing room. No sign of Charity, so she tried the library, knocking first. There was no response, so she pushed open the door to find Randolph perched on the window ledge, staring out over the snow-covered garden, cradling a glass containing what looked like whisky. He twisted to face her when she entered.

Emma dipped a curtsy. "I apologise for the intrusion, Lord Brackley. I am looking for Lady Charity. Have you seen her perchance?"

"Not since last night. Are *you* not her companion? As such, I presume you are here to assist *her*, not fritter the days away at your leisure. Surely, you are expected to be privy to Lady Charity's whereabouts at all times?" His tone brusque and somewhat accusatory.

Emma gawked at him. *What the dickens was his problem? She was not answerable to him.* Truth be told she was not even answerable to Charity. Her position in the Driffield household was unpaid — she was given a roof over her head, and food, in exchange for acting as a buffer between Charity and her father. Today was the first time in nearly four years she had visited a modiste. The clothes she wore day in and day out, were those she managed to pack before leaving Aspley Manor. Her lovely afternoon faded with her smile, and her brow lowered.

"I fail to see what business it is of yours as to what or to whom I am or am not privy. I simply asked a question, all I required was a civil answer. How foolish of me. I should have realised such a thing is beyond you. Good day, my lord." She spun on her heel and flounced out of the room. Forgetting where she was, Emma slammed the door closed, her temper bubbling. Marching upstairs, she met Charity coming out of her bedchamber.

"Emma there you are. Where have you been all afternoon, I needed you."

"I sincerely doubt that, my lady," Emma growled. She shoved open the door to her own bedchamber, banging that one closed behind her for good measure, leaving an astounded Charity staring after her, mouth agape.

CHAPTER 7

*M*eanwhile, back in the library, a suitably chastened Randolph was rubbing his chin. *The devil, he did not handle that well, at all.* Bloody Emma Newbury was a thorn in his side. No matter what he did, she was always there, teasing at the edge of his consciousness — possibly prompting his incautious outburst. Three nights past, Randolph had come face-to-face with Felicity for the first time since hearing of her marriage. She was eager to engage him in conversation but, to his surprise, he had no desire to linger in her company, so simply wished her well and continued on his way. He wanted to share this revelation with someone, and despite their scant encounters, it was Emma he wanted to tell — somehow, he knew she would understand.

Even when escorting Charity to whatever social event she wished to attend, Emma was with him. A silent shadow dogging his every move. Her dark eyes searching his face, her svelte figure taunting him, and that persistent notion he ought to recognise her — he wished he could recall from where. He had wracked his brains, but it continued to elude him. He kept meaning to ask Nathaniel, but Charity was dominating all his free time.

The look on Emma's face when he upbraided her — and she *was* correct, it was none of his business — made his chest pinch. That he was the one who caused her happy smile to vanish gave him pause. *What the hell was he doing?*

It was the evening of the ball. Emma's stomach was a mass of knots. Jane was assisting her into one of the new dresses, all of which arrived that morning. It had been difficult to choose, each one was exquisite. She may be the daughter of a viscount, but Emma had never owned anything as eye-catching as these gowns, and a frisson of excitement ran through her when she stroked the fine material.

Eventually, she decided on a floor-length creation in ice blue silk. The delicate lace overlay, in a slightly darker hue, drifted to the floor at the back to form a short train. At the front, it draped open in a v from the centre of the high waist, revealing an insert of filmy chiffon scattered with an intricate design. Finely stitched in a subtle shade of burnished gold, the pattern was repeated in the trim around the neckline, and echoed in the lace and silk circling her waist.

Jane twisted and pulled Emma's riotous curls into a simple yet elegant bun, leaving one or two ringlets loose to frame her face. White elbow-length gloves; soft, low-heeled leather shoes, and a fan completed the outfit. It was a masquerade ball, and Juliette had lent her guest a gorgeous mask in silver, which covered nearly the whole of her face, disguising her features — to Emma's relief.

Walking over to the long mirror next to the wardrobe, Emma did a double-take. "Why, Jane, thank you! I do not think my own mother would recognise me. I had no idea I could look so… ladylike."

"Go on with you, Miss. You are always ladylike, which is more than I can sa—" Jane clamped her mouth shut. It was not done to disparage a visitor, however much you might want to. Emma chuckled.

"Fret not, Jane, I understand." She sighed. "I should not be going to this ball."

Jane, who had heard all about Emma's past — Charity's two maids were inveterate gossips — tutted. "Of course, you should. You are as entitled to attend as anyone else. Go on, have some fun. You deserve it." Grinning at Emma's valiant attempt to look enthusiastic.

Juliette and Nathaniel were waiting in the hall, and both turned when Emma descended the stairs. Charity had gone ahead with Randolph, taking Evelyn, her personal maid, as chaperone.

Emma smothered her mirth at their matching expressions of astonishment; it was rather nice to render people speechless.

Juliette recovered first. "Emma, you look beautiful. That gown is sublime." Smiling in delight, while Jane draped Emma's cloak around her shoulders and then handed her the fan. "Now, let us make haste. We are about to turn some heads." Taking Nathaniel's proffered arm, Juliette led the way to the carriage, and before long they had arrived, shed their cloaks, and were being announced by a smartly uniformed steward.

Emma was held immobile by the scene in front of her. The ball was at the city residence of the Duke and Duchess of Droitwich, a house of monumental proportions, and decorated as befitted the occasion. Below her, at the foot of the ornately carved imperial staircase, a sea of people mingled; the tinkle of crystal, lilting laughter, and the buzz of conversation, both familiar and daunting. Strains of music wafted through a pair of glass doors standing open at the far side of the reception area, and Emma thought she could see the whirl of gowns as couples danced. Every surface was polished until it gleamed, reflecting colour and light from the abundance of flower arrangements and the multitude of candelabra. Gilt-edged mirrors, placed strategically around the walls, created the illusion that the room was twice its size.

For a split second, Emma wanted to flee. It was an age since she had been to a ball. *What if she had forgotten the dance steps? What if no one asked her to dance...? How mortifying. No, it would be better if no one asked her to dance, that way she would not make a fool of herself.* She sucked in a steadying breath, recognising she was giving in to unreasonable panic. Then Juliette was there, tucking her arm under Emma's and ushering her along to the ballroom, Nathaniel on their heels.

They found Ged and Melissa, engaged in conversation with two other couples to whom Juliette introduced Emma, and whose names Emma immediately forgot. There was no point consigning them to memory, she would be leaving in a few weeks, unlikely to return.

"Would you care to dance?" Ged asked Emma after the group had been chatting for a few minutes, a cheerful smile warming his sombre face. Emma glanced at Melissa, who inclined her head and waved her fan.

"Please dance with him, it will save my poor foot." Melissa

grinned at her betrothed's mock affronted expression. "I promise to take a turn on the floor with you later."

Holding Melissa's gaze, Ged lifted her hand and kissed her wrist. To Emma, it seemed an unspoken message passed between them, and she looked away, unwilling to intrude on so private a moment. A wave of intense longing swept over her; to have a man stare at her with such ardour was something she doubted she would ever experience. If she ever married, it would probably be for convenience, not love. Unexpectedly, Randolph's face wafted through her mind, and her heartbeat quickened. *Why did he insist on popping into her head at the most inopportune times?* Unable to answer her own question, she ignored it and focused on the evening ahead. Placing her hand on Ged's arm, she moved with him to the dance floor.

CHAPTER 8

*A*cross the room, Randolph was talking with a group of friends when he heard familiar voices. Glancing up he saw Nate and... wait was that Ged... dancing? Surely not? He never left Melissa and — mask aside — the woman he was dancing with was most certainly *not* Melissa. Brow creased in puzzlement, Randolph scanned the room to see Melissa and Juliette gossiping animatedly with two other couples, Nate strolling towards them with a tray of drinks. *Who the devil was that woman?*

He watched as she danced. She was very light on her feet, her body swaying in time with the music, her dress flowing around her as she moved; glossy hair piled on her head, and her face hidden behind a silvery mask. She was chatting with Ged, making him smile, and Randolph felt a tug of something in his gut. If he did not know better, he would say it was jealousy, but that was not possible, he had no idea who she was. Then, Ged spun her, and the woman no longer had her back to Randolph.

By chance, their eyes collided.

She faltered, and in a flash, he knew.

Good lord, it was Emma!

When the dance ended, of their own volition, Randolph's feet took him across the room, where Emma was bobbing a curtsy to Ged's bow. She was a little breathless as she thanked his friend, and they were about to leave the floor when he reached them.

"May I beg the next dance?" he cut in. Emma paused, but did not turn. "Please?" The uncharacteristic entreaty in his tone made both Emma and Ged do a slow about face. Ged's expression held a warning, but Randolph sent him a look, one he knew Ged would understand, relieved to see a slight inclination of his friend's head. Emma looked sceptical, their last clash no doubt playing on her mind. She sent a dubious glance at Ged, who smiled at her, nodded, then walked over to rejoin Melissa who was sitting with Juliette at the edge of the dance floor.

Emma waited, fidgeting a little. The music started; it was a waltz. Her head shot up and Randolph detected consternation in her dark gaze.

"No, 'tis a waltz. You should be… Charity…" she waved her hand distractedly. Randolph caught and held it, placing his other hand on her waist.

"I do not wish to dance with Charity. I wish to dance with you."

"Why?" she demanded baldly.

"You intrigue me," was all he said and whisked her around the floor. Emma desperately tried to make eye contact with Juliette and Melissa, but they were engrossed in conversation. Biting her lip, she tried to calm her nerves and enjoy the dance.

Randolph was staring down at the woman he now clasped. This was the first time he had danced with a lady as tall as Emma, astounded at how perfectly she fitted into his arms. When he danced with Charity, he felt awkward and ungainly; with Emma, he felt as though they were floating. It came to him, that if he held her close, he could rest his cheek on her hair. *Wait... where did **that** come from?* He shook his head to dispel the image, but it lingered, and as he looked down at her pale face, spying a sprinkle of freckles and the dusky curve of her eyelashes, just visible beneath the mask, he was possessed with an ardent desire to kiss her senseless in the middle of the dance floor. Only his arrangement with Charity, and the fact he had no mind to confuse an already convoluted situation prevented him.

Bloody hell.

Somehow, without trying, and in less than three weeks, Emma Newbury had inveigled her way into his heart.

Now, what was he going to do?

Emma concentrated on not muddling the steps of the waltz, keeping her gaze firmly fixed on Randolph's waistcoat. Distractedly, she noticed it was a beautiful waistcoat. Rich, bronze brocade — matching his cravat — over a white shirt, his tailcoat and pants such a dark brown they were almost black. She could see the rise and fall of his chest beneath the fine material and felt her breathing hitch as, out of the blue, she imagined running her fingers over his skin. She swallowed on a gulp which sounded like a strangled hiccup.

"Are you quite well, Miss Newbury?" Randolph murmured solicitously, while they executed a flawless turn.

"Errr... y-yes, thank you... I just..." Emma let that trail off. She had nothing coherent to say — better to keep quiet. For a little longer she relaxed and let the magic of the waltz wash over her. The dance came to an end, far too quickly for both Randolph and Emma, not that either was prepared to admit it. Emma thanked him, dipped a curtsy and fled, needing to put some space between herself and this tall, taciturn, devastatingly handsome gentleman who, until ten minutes ago, she presumed found her a nuisance.

As Randolph watched her go, realisation slammed into him, causing him to palm his forehead. He was doing *exactly* what he accused Ged of, no more than three months ago. Treating life as a game. There was the game of shadows he played, working in a covert capacity for Lucas Withers — that was acceptable, nay necessary. Then there was the game he was playing with Charity. It had been amusing, and he took gleeful satisfaction not only in flaunting Charity in front of Felicity, but also aiding the former gain the undivided attention of young Fitzroy.

The fun had begun to pall, leaving him peculiarly empty and a little disquieted. Which led, uncomfortably, to the game he was playing with romance. The affection he had harboured for Felicity was trifling compared with the myriad of emotions Emma elicited. With barely a glance she could make his heart triple its beat; when she was near, he had to employ every vestige of will power not to drag her against him and kiss her into a ferment. Yet, she seemed indifferent to him, a predicament doubtless exacerbated by his churlish attitude.

It was quite simple really — if he lost her, the game was over. Nothing else mattered, not even their difference in status. He had to win, he had to win Emma, win her heart, win her soul, but this game followed a different set of rules; one wrong move and he would lose her, and he did not know where to begin.

He needed help.

CHAPTER 9

*H*uffing a frustrated sigh, he traipsed over to where Ged and Nate were standing.

"Care to explain?" Ged asked.

"Not sure I can," Randolph confessed, his head whirling.

"Are we to assume Miss Newbury is at the root of your… errr… quandary?" Nate posited. Randolph gaped at his two friends, seeing Emma's face superimposed over theirs. *Dark brown, her eyes were a velvety dark brown, like hot chocolate before the milk was added*. He sank onto a convenient chair and dropped his head into his hands.

"How did you guess? Never mind. I do not know what to do. I hardly know her, but dammit all, I cannot stop thinking about her. Thing is, a few days after they arrived, Charity was complaining to me about Emma. I agreed because it was easier than suffering Charity's displeasure, although, to be fair, I was not quite so brutal in my comments," he added, absently, "Charity called Emma plain, which I should have refuted, for she is breathtakingly beautiful. Unfortunately, Emma was reading on the window seat and overheard." Unbidden, he recalled Emma's bleak countenance. Dragging his mind back to the present, he went on, "Anyway, she was righteously aggrieved, and then I was abominably rude to her two days past. She asked a simple question and I all but bit her head off, demanded to know what she thought she was doing gadding about when she should be tending to Charity."

Ged and Nate glanced at each other, half-concerned half-amused. It seemed Randolph had met his match.

"Yet she danced with you," Nate remarked.

"I did not give her much choice."

"She had every opportunity to walk away," Ged interjected. "And I do not think she is as unmoved by you as you suppose. Why not go and find her? Maybe explain why you have been so cantankerous."

"I do not know how." Randolph shrugged his shoulders, helplessly.

"Oh, I think you do." Ged grinned. "I recall a certain conversation at Nate's wedding when you were quite vociferous about falling in love. Apply that to your own situation. Yes..." he raised a palm, "...I know you escorted Charity here tonight, but if you take a quick look to your left — don't make it obvious man — young Fitzroy is ushering her onto the dance floor. Mayhap your ploy had the desired effect."

Randolph glanced casually where Ged indicated, to see Charity with Lord Spencer. Observing the couple, he felt a weight rolling off him; with luck, this would release him from their pact. At the same instant, another thought came to him.

"Nate, have I, have we met Miss Newbury before? I am dashed if can pin it down, but I am certain our paths have crossed." To his amazement, Ged and Nate burst out laughing.

"Oh Randi, you are hopeless. How you managed to retain all that vital information in your brain yet can forget a pretty face is beyond me. Mayhap if Miss Newbury was a confidential document, you would not have this trouble."

"We *do* know her, then? Put me out of my misery, 'tis driving me to distraction."

"Why did you not ask?

"I intended to, never got around to it. Didn't think it mattered. Turns out it does."

"Before I tell you, answer me two questions. You have fallen in love with an impecunious lady's companion. Do you wish to marry her, or bed her?"

"Both." His reply was instant. Ged tried not to grin at Randolph's red face.

"Second, will Lady Felicity's betrayal affect the way you treat Emma?"

"No!" Randolph all but shouted. "God no. Since meeting Emma, I have not given Felicity a second thought." His expression and the shuddering breath he drew, did more to convince Nate than his friend's words. "Tell me who she is."

Taking pity on him, Nate said, "Do you recall the three of us investigating Viscount Aspley? It was… oh… two years gone June. We spent a couple of days at the Aspley estate in Somerset." The two men watched as the cogs in Randolph's brain began to tumble. "We were working our way through the papers in the study, with Charity's father, when the daughter of the late Viscount offered us refreshments."

Randolph sifted through information in his head, finding the day in question. Suddenly, all those vague little details and snatches of memory clicked into place. He remembered locking eyes with a vexed young madam, as well as being surprised at the reproach which followed.

"That was Emma!" It was a statement not a question.

Nate and Ged nodded.

"Yes, it was," Nate affirmed. "Now, I suggest you find her, apologise for your crass behaviour and see whether she might forgive you," chuckling at Randolph's glower. "Go on, before 'tis too late and someone else swoops her up."

That was threat enough. Randolph thanked his friends and disappeared in the same direction Emma fled less than fifteen minutes previously.

Ged and Nate watched him go.

"Let us hope he does not botch this up," Ged commented sagely. Nate agreed, as they were drawn back into conversation with their womenfolk.

Emma was in the colonnaded walkway just outside the ballroom, leaning against a fluted column. It was a frigid night, but she was scarcely aware, lost in contemplation, while simultaneously enthralled by the ethereal wonder of the winter's night. The sounds from the ball were muted here. The familiar cadence of light-hearted merriment — reminiscent of musical notes — along with the glow from what she suspected must be thousands of candles spilling through the numerous windows, was so very inviting. Subtle temptations to rejoin the festive throng.

She resisted. If she went back inside, she would see Randolph dancing with Charity, and she had not quite regained enough composure for that just yet.

Instead, she tilted her head to admire the crystal-clear sky, a veil of stars twinkling in its inky depths. The pale moon, climbing slowly to its zenith, illuminated London in pearly radiance and made the pristine snow in the garden below her sparkle as though lit from within.

Emma sighed.

This was perfection.

Well almost.

Perfection would be if she could share so spectacular a

view with someone she loved. *Head out of the clouds, girl*, she admonished, *he is not for the likes of you*. Regardless of whether her father was posthumously vindicated, it was too late. Charity had her claws in him, and that was that.

Emma descended the three steps to the terrace, pausing for a moment, unable to stop a stray tear from trickling down her cheek — unaware the opening of a door bathed her in a shaft of soft candlelight.

Randolph eventually tracked Emma to the garden, somewhat bemused as to why she would leave the warmth of the house but determined this evening would not end without him clearing the air between them. Maybe then she might believe his other, far more important, revelation.

Soundlessly, he opened the door and scanned the walkway. He could not see anyone, not even a shadow, and thinking she must have gone back in, was about to retrace his steps when something made him look down. There she was, her hair glimmering in the light from the doorway, face half-hidden under the silvery mask.

About to speak, to warn her of his presence, he hesitated, detecting a solitary tear roll down her cheek, catching the reflection from the countless candles flickering behind him. While his heart ached for her sadness, it gave him the courage to close the door, and follow her into the night.

CHAPTER 10

*E*mma heard the creak of the French doors but did not turn. Plenty of guests had ventured out, only to declare it much too frosty, scurrying back into the warmth. Revelling in the silence, she strolled towards an elegant folly. It stood several feet to the right of the terrace… far enough from the house, that it was unlikely she would be disturbed. She was about to sink onto the cold grey stone of the steps, when an unexpected voice arrested her.

"Why did you run?"

She spun around tripping on her gown, only Randolph's strong arm steadied her.

"T-thank you, my lord." She peered at him and pondered his question. "Why do you care?"

"I asked first. If you answer my question, I promise to answer yours."

Emma frowned. This was a peculiar sort of conversation in a duke's garden, at midnight in the middle of winter. On the brink of tossing out a flippant repost, something about his watchful gaze made Emma rephrase her reply.

"Because I do not want your pity."

Randolph smiled a slow, tender smile, and her insides turned to slush.

"I do not pity you, Miss Emma Newbury. There are many things I feel for you, not one of them is pity." He stroked one finger along her jaw and saw her eyelashes sweep down, heard her breathing hitch.

Wary of where this was going, Emma lifted her eyes to his. "Your turn."

"I care because I want another dance with you, I want every dance to be with you. I care because since the moment we met, your face refuses to leave my thoughts. I care because—"

"Charity…" Emma interrupted curtly, ignoring the flutter of hope coiling in her stomach.

"…is of no consequence." He felt Emma start to pull away and tightened his hold. "Wait, let me finish. We were simply facilitating the other's cause. Charity wanted Lord Fitzroy to notice her, and I wanted to prove to the very new Lady Westmorland, whom I had been courting, her precipitous marriage did not wound me."

"You are in love with Lady Westmorland?" The tiny spark died. Emma rubbed her forehead. *Why was he telling her this?*

Carefully removing Emma's mask, Randolph placed it on the top of the stone post and, greatly daring, took her hand. "No, I am not in love with Lady Westmorland. For a time, I thought I was and was incensed at what I considered to be her cold-blooded betrayal. She did not even have the decency to inform me of her impending marriage, leaving me to find out the day *after* her nuptials. I got very drunk and behaved like a fatwit for several days until Nate and Ged dunked me in the Livingston's pond." He offered a rueful grin when he spotted Emma trying not to laugh at the image his words conjured up. "Go on laugh… I deserve it."

"No one deserves to be made a fool of."

Randolph heard the echo of long suppressed anguish in her statement, and he wanted nothing more than to obliterate any memory of such sorrow.

In the midst of her confusion, Emma realised his hand still held hers and his thumb was rubbing her gloved palm. So simple a gesture, yet it sent ribbons of heat right through her, robbing her of coherent thought.

Clinging to her rapidly evaporating senses, she added, "I'm afraid I do not understand what any of this has to do with me."

Randolph ran his free hand through his hair. For a man erudite in matters of covert operations and classified investigations, in matters of the heart, he felt like a philistine. He tucked an errant strand of hair behind her ear and gave it his best shot.

"I am very glad she married that oaf, for had she not, I might have missed out on meeting you, and that would have been a travesty. Emma, you captivate and enchant me, your body bewitches me, your smile, although too rare, beguiles me, and your eyes? I could drown in your eyes. That said, I know your impression of me is poor. I have been discourteous, nay, unkind on more than one occasion. My only excuse is that I was stubbornly trying to deny the one thing that was blindingly obvious, had I the sense to stop fighting, and acknowledge it."

Emma stood motionless, her head on one side, staring at him, her face unreadable, but Randolph felt her gripping his hand as though it was a lifeline.

Emma heard his words. They were fine words, actually, they were wonderful words — eloquent and sincere, but what good were they? Despite her background, her heritage, and even given the probability her family's standing would be restored, she was no longer part of Society. Any association with her would be frowned upon; his family would not approve. Did he want her as his mistress? If he asked, she would say no, much as she might want to. To be intimate with him, to know him completely then to watch while he wed another would destroy her. Before she could formulate an intelligent question, Randolph spoke again, his voice enveloping her, tangible as an embrace.

"Emma, I love you. My greatest wish is to marry you."

There they were, the words she longed to hear.

Could she trust them?

She shivered, and it was naught to do with the winter's air.

The spark caught and held, the flame began to burn.

Emma leant back slightly, the better to study his face. His expression left her in no doubt, but...

"Will it be enough?" Her whispered plea tore at his heart. He was not naive, conscious they faced obstacles, but if she loved him half as much as he loved her, he knew they could surmount every single one.

"If you are with me, it will be more than enough." He drew her close and, letting go of her hand, tucked her against him. Her body moulded to his as precisely as though they were two halves of a whole. "I love you so much, I would gladly give up everything, rather than let you go."

"Randolph, I love you too. I think I fell in love with you before I ever knew what love was. One summer's day..."

"In a quiet study, where four men were systematically dismantling your life?"

Emma's mouth fell open in shock. "You remember?"

He kissed her forehead. "I admit, it has taken some time. I suspected we had met but could not fathom from where. I assumed it was some social gathering. I confess Nate provided the final link after you and I danced... and no," as Emma, again, tried to disentangle herself, "that makes no difference." He explained Nate's questions. "If you do not believe me, he will be more than happy to confirm it."

"I believe you."

"Please, will you marry me?" He kissed her nose. One hand stroking up her spine to cup her neck.

"What of your family, your friends?" A delicious raft of sensations began a leisurely glissade up her body. "Oh my..." when he kissed her behind the ear.

"I do not want to marry them."

Emma giggled, which quickly became a gasp when his lips ghosted along her throat. "Randolph..."

"Yes, my love." Kissing the corner of her mouth.

"Ask me again. 'Tis the most beautiful question I ever heard."

"Emma Newbury, love of my life, thief of my heart, will you marry me?"

"Randolph Craythorpe, after giving your proposal a *lot* of thought..." then, seeing his face crinkle with amusement, Emma shrugged, unrepentantly, "...fine, seconds, I gave it seconds of thought. Would you like me to take longer?" Pertly. He shook his head, a wicked grin forming on his sinfully seductive lips. "I think perhaps I will." She feigned a resigned sigh, "'Tis clear you cannot be left to your own devices."

"Is that a yes?" Randolph cupped her face in his chilled hands.

"Yes." Emma smiled then, a gloriously, unrestrained, joyful smile.

Randolph kissed her. He kissed her until the freezing winter's night felt more like a summer heatwave, until she swore the heavenly host had arrived three days early, until she did not care who came upon them in a snowy garden in one of the most eminent houses in London.

The sensation was no longer nameless.

EPILOGUE

A YEAR LATER

*E*arly January in London. The undulating whiteness covering the ground glistened in the weak, wintry sunshine, and while the morning was currently bright, clouds were building, their yellowish hue a harbinger of more snow.

The air was still — only a few hardy birds twittered, their cheerful trill alleviating the silence. Despite the cold, a tall, dark-haired woman, snug in a blood-red woollen wrap was sitting on a bench just outside a set of glass doors.

The last few weeks had been hectic. Close friends had visited during the festive season and, although she loved them dearly, it was a blessed relief to revert to her tranquil, rather mundane everyday existence.

Standing, she brushed down her skirts, and strolled into the quaint garden, along the gravel paths cleared only that morning by Jeb, their trusted gardener.

She trailed her fingers over the neat row of hardy rosemary bushes — inhaling the soothing fragrance — their feathery leaves offering a splash of green against the white background. There was something magical, almost otherworldly about snowy gardens, and they never failed to evoke the memory of the night her husband proposed.

A hint of a smile curved her lips as images from that evening drifted through her mind. Theirs had been an unusual romance; his proposal came before their courtship. She was the oldest daughter of a once disgraced viscount, he the oldest son of a marquis.

By Society's rules, by long-standing convention, theirs was a love doomed. He had much more to lose by declaring his suit, and she feared there would be rumours she tricked him into marriage.

She had no idea how or why, but none of that happened — unaware, at the time, of exactly who he worked for or the influence his superiors wielded.

They married three months later.

She heard footsteps and turned to see her husband striding towards her.

"Emma, what on earth are you doing out here? 'Tis icy."

"Savouring the quiet," she smiled up at him; tall as she was, he towered over her.

He chuckled. "It is rather blissful to be just the two of us once more." He kissed her nose and wrapped his arms around her, pillowing his cheek on her head.

Emma was endlessly amazed that the sheer strength of feeling they shared had not dimmed one iota; that the love, the tenderness and the passion burned as fiercely, as the first time they kissed, and, in fact, had deepened.

"We have the whole day to ourselves..." she let that dangle, grinning mischievously.

"What did you have in mind?"

"Well..." she tapped her cheek, pretending to contemplate, "...we could take a constitutional, build a snowman, read..." her suggestions effectively cut off when a pair of irresistibly sensuous lips covered hers. "R-rand—"

"Emma?" he moulded her against him, hands swarming under her wrap, teasing at the buttons on the back of her gown.

"Randolph, the staff," her voice catching, as his lips blazed a path across her cool skin.

"I do not wish to kiss the staff."

"You really are the most audacious man," her words finishing on a breathy moan, aware her gown was beginning to slither from her shoulders. "Randolph, while I admit making love in the snow might seem attractive, we shall both freeze. Be sensible."

"Fine." Ignoring Emma's squeak of protest, he slung her over his shoulder as though she weighed nothing, and carried her up the steps into the library, chuckling at her futile effort to wriggle free.

"Randolph!"

"Hush."

He kicked the door closed behind him before depositing her on the large chaise by the fire. Circling the room, he locked both doors then stood, gazing at his wife, who was delectably dishevelled. Her dress had slipped, exposing the rise of her breast. His heart thudded.

"Randolph... we have a bedchamber," Emma chided, making no attempt to move.

"And waste a perfectly good chaise? Oh, my love, surely you jest?" Randolph closed the gap between them, his manner — predatory, and Emma felt the thrill of anticipation ripple down her spine.

With tortuous deliberation, he divested her of her gown, then her delicate undergarments, struggling to maintain his control when Emma returned the favour. Naked, hands and lips flying over heated skin — pleasure heightening, they tumbled off the chaise onto the rug in front of the fire.

Outside, the snow began to fall. Slowly and gently at first

— tiny flakes floating to the ground. The breeze picked up, whipping them into a frenzied swirl; innumerable, exquisitely formed, lacy fragments spinning chaotically from the greying sky.

Their mesmerising dance mirrored the ardour spiralling out of control in a peaceful library, in an elegant townhouse, in the middle of winter, in London.

Love is not a game, and there are no rules — in order to triumph, you must surrender.

In winning Emma, Randolph lost his heart — a forfeit he willingly paid.

EXCERPT FROM THE HIGHWAYMAN'S KISS

SURRENDERED HEARTS - BOOK 1

*J*uliette St Clair had never had anything exciting happen to her. Well, to be scrupulously honest, a tiny voice in her head chastised her, there was that one incident — oh and remember the night *he* nearly, almost kissed you. No, Juliette countered — refusing to allow herself the indulgence of recalling the bliss of that moment, her internal debate agitated now — placing the blame firmly on too much wine or the moonlight or some such fancy. Getting back to her point, in the great scheme of things, she could count on the fingers of one hand the things she could genuinely describe as exciting.

Juliette spent a few days each week helping her Papa, acting as a secretary of sorts, the remainder saw her buried in books or visiting the museum or — if she really had to — attending the occasional garden party. Her evenings were filled with musical soirees, the theatre or any one of the innumerable balls to which she chaperoned her younger sister, Letitia; whiling away the time, bored witless and ignored, while Letitia was danced off her feet by handsome young bucks.

. . .

Until the day she was robbed by a highwayman!

It was early afternoon and still at least three hours until their carriage would reach the inn where they intended to spend the night. They had barely even started the journey and already Letitia and Faith were arguing. They always argued; Juliette had long since shut her ears to their blathering, lost in contemplation of the previous three months. She was travelling, along with her mother and two of her sisters, home to London, having spent three weeks at Highdene, the country estate of her uncle, Lord Walthamstowe. She loved her uncle dearly, but he tended to manage people and Juliette hated being managed.

A hint of a whisper of scandal clung to Juliette and, although most had forgotten — it happened during her first Season, the matter almost immediately pushed aside by the next rumour — there were those who took cruel delight in reminding her she was still single after five Seasons. Her uncle had made a suggestion; one he believed would put an end to it. Juliette knew it was false hope; neither did she wish to wed someone twenty years her senior, a man she scarcely knew and, following his behaviour after dinner two nights previously, was determined not to.

For the most part Juliette no longer heard the malicious murmurings; although, every now and then, she pondered how different her life might have been had she let *him* have his way, that evening five years ago. With the gift of hindsight, she accepted it would have been a troubled match. He wanted to control her, and she was too independently minded to allow that, but such issues were common amongst the *ton*, and there were few in her circle who married for love. She was aware men took mistresses, their wives content to enjoy the trappings of wealth. Even though such a life appeared to offer the measure of security many women craved, Juliette was not prepared to settle for anything less than love and, of late, another had begun to show interest. For the first time since that awful night, she dared to hope.

Despite a less than auspicious first meeting — she hadn't received his attentions with much grace — he seemed to enjoy her company, deliberately seeking her out. He was quite the most handsome man she had ever laid eyes on and that almost kiss…a smile curved Juliette's mouth as she recalled the brush of his lips on hers, tingles ran along her spine even now, weeks after. She shook her head trying to dismiss the sensation, but it lurked on the edge of her consciousness, tantalising her. In truth it was quite confusing. What happened now? Did he really care for her, or was it her imagination? She hadn't seen him for nigh on a month; he might have forgotten her already, the mere idea making her heart ache.

Determined not to dwell on it — there was nothing she could do about it here, miles from anywhere — Juliette dragged her attention back to her family, two of whom were still quarrelling.

Moments later a shout rang out and their carriage came to a violent halt, jerking the four within off their seats. There was a kerfuffle of men and voices, and before they could register what was happening the four women were out of the coach, two masked men rifling through their belongings, while a third stood guard over their driver.

Covertly, Juliette observed them; grateful, for once, she was wearing her spectacles. So, this was what highwaymen looked like? She recalled several articles in the papers her father took regarding a spate of hold ups across the region.

The most mysterious thing being that even when items of value were stolen, they turned up at the owner's residence days later, neatly wrapped in cloth and undamaged.

Something about the three men tickled at Juliette's memory, although, she couldn't put her finger on what it was. She had never seen a highwayman before, but something didn't ring quite true. She ran her eyes over them, noting their bearing, their attire and their speech patterns. There was nothing rough or uncultured about these men, they didn't look desperate or ruthless and they were certainly cleaner than she expected any vagabond to be. Then one of them, the tallest of the three made a careless gesture and something clicked in Juliette's brain.

She stepped forward...

ABOUT THE AUTHOR

Rosie Chapel lives in Perth, Australia with her hubby and three furkids. When not writing, she loves catching up with friends, burying herself in a book (or three), discovering the wonders of Western Australia, or — and the best — a quiet evening at home with her husband, enjoying a glass of wine and a movie.

Website http://rosiechapel.com/

ALSO BY ROSIE CHAPEL

Historical Fiction

The Hannah's Heirloom Sequence

The Pomegranate Tree - Book One

Echoes of Stone and Fire - Book Two

Embers of Destiny - Book Three

Etched in Starlight - Prequel

Hannah's Heirloom Trilogy - Compilation – e-book only

Prelude to Fate

Regency Romances

The Linen and Lace Series

Once Upon An Earl - Book One

To Unlock Her Heart - Book Two

Love on a Winter's Tide - Book Three

A Love Unquenchable - Book Four

A Hidden Rose - Book Five

The Daffodil Garden

The Unconventional Duchess

Rescuing Her Knight

His Fiery Hoyden

A Regency Duet

A Regency Christmas Double

Fate is Curious

A Christmas Prayer *with Ashlee Shades*

The Lady's Wager

Winning Emma

A Love Impossible

Unravelling Roana

Fairy Tale Romance

Chasing Bluebells

Contemporary Romances

Of Ruins and Romance

All At Once It's You

Cobweb Dreams

Just One Step

His Heart's Second Sigh

The Pomegranate Tree

Hannah's Heirloom - Book One

Hoping to trace the origins of an ancient ruby clasp, a gift from her long dead grandmother, Hannah Wilson travels to the fortress of Masada with her best friend, Max. Strange dreams concerning a rebel ambush begin to haunt Hannah and following a tragic accident, she slips into the world of Ancient Masada.

A woman out of time, Hannah must rely on her instincts and her knowledge of what will befall this citadel to survive. Will she escape, or is she doomed to die along with hundreds of others as Masada falls – and what does any of this have to do with an ancient ruby clasp?

Echoes of Stone and Fire

Hannah's Heirloom - Book Two

Pompeii - a vibrant city lost in time following the AD79 eruption of Vesuvius. Now rediscovered, archaeologists yearn for an opportunity to uncover the town's past. Some things, however, are best left alone - revealing the secrets hidden beneath the stones could prove perilous. Hannah and Max are brought to Pompeii by a surprise invitation to join an excavation team who are trying to uncover the city's long history.

After entering an excavated house that bears a Hebrew inscription, Hannah's two worlds collide, and she falls back through time to ancient Pompeii. A place where her ancestor is a physician to gladiators engaged in mortal combat, where riotous mobs run amok and where a ghost from the past returns to haunt her.

Will Hannah and her loved ones manage to escape the devastation she knows is coming, before the town is engulfed in volcanic ash?

Will she ever find her way back to Max the love of her life, waiting not so patiently millennia away? Or will echoes be all that remain?

Embers of Destiny

Hannah's Heirloom - Book Three

AD80 - Hannah and Maxentius must embark on a new journey to Northern Britannia. This harsh frontier is far from the comforts of Rome and danger lurks where least expected; a garrison of soldiers, some unhappy with their isolated posting; local tribes, outwardly accepting of their Roman occupier, but who may still resent the seizure of their lands.

Millennia away, Hannah Vallier finds a familiar item while working in a museum near Hadrian's Wall. It is the pomegranate; carved by Maxentius on Masada. Before Hannah can discuss it with Max, disaster strikes! Believing her husband has been killed, Hannah retreats into the past, her soul melding with that of her ancestor, but with little idea of what they could face. Is the risk from the conquered tribes, or much closer to home?

As rebellion threatens to shatter a fragile peace, Hannah's heart whispers that just maybe Max isn't dead and that he is calling her home. Can she trust her heart, or will she remain caught out of time, her destiny floating away like embers on a breeze?

Etched in Starlight

Hannah's Heirloom - Prequel

Maxentius - a Roman soldier fresh from the battlefields of Armenia, arrives to take command of the military outpost of Masada, Herod's isolated citadel in the Judaean desert. A seemingly mundane posting after years of warfare, Maxentius finds it more challenging to maintain a focused garrison than to face the wrath of the Parthians across a disputed frontier.

Hannah - a young Hebrew physician spends her days dealing with injuries from street brawls, deprivation, disease and loss. As her beloved Jerusalem plunges into chaos; her brother — who belongs to a band of rebels determined to drive out their Roman occupiers — tells her of their plans to storm a desert fortress and steal the weapons stored there, persuading his reluctant sister to go with him.

Masada - following the ambush, Hannah finds and treats three badly wounded Roman soldiers. In the aftermath and against impossible odds, Hannah and Maxentius realise that they are more than healer and captive, their fate already etched in starlight.

Prelude to Fate

For Lucia, staring into the jaws of an horrific death, escape seems impossible.

Rufius Atellus, a veteran Roman soldier, is appalled when he recognises one of the victims about to be executed. Surely this is a ghastly mistake?

A ferocious she-wolf, anticipating a tasty meal, suddenly finds herself under a human's control.

In an unexpected twist, and as danger threatens, the lives of all three become inextricably entwined.

Was it chance brought them together in that theatre of bloodshed, or simply a prelude to fate?

REGENCY ROMANCES

Once Upon An Earl

Linen and Lace - Book One

When Fate saw fit to intervene in the life of Giles Trevallier, the very respectable Earl of Winchester, by dropping a female — soaked to the skin and with no memory of who she is or how she came to be there — literally at his feet, no one could have predicted the outcome.

While uncovering her identity, Giles realises he is falling hopelessly in love with his mystery guest, who unbeknownst to him, is succumbing to similar emotions; but, when the heart is involved, a thoughtless word or gesture can thwart even Fate's best-laid plans.

Faced with misunderstandings, whispers of scandal, secret documents and foreign agents, their chance at a happy ever after seems elusive, but fairy tales often happen when least expected, and love — however inconvenient — usually finds a way to conquer all.

To Unlock Her Heart

Linen and Lace - Book Two

Abused by a duke, and shunned by Society, relief seems at hand when Grace Aldeburgh is bequeathed a house in a small village, far from malicious gossips.

Once there, a tentative friendship blooms between Grace and Theo Elliott, the local doctor, who has already resolved to be the man to unlock her heart.

Just when happiness appears to be within her grasp, her erstwhile tormentor once again stalks Grace. After a failed kidnap attempt, the duke's quest culminates in an acrimonious confrontation, and the reason for his venal pursuit becomes agonisingly clear.

Love on a Winter's Tide

Linen and Lace - Book Three

Every day, Helena disappears into a world few acknowledge, helping the poor, downtrodden, and abused. A husband is the last thing she can be bothered with.

Busy managing his shipping line, Hugh Drummond sees no need for a wife, whose only joy is dancing and frivolity. If — and it was a huge if — he ever married, it would be to a woman as capable as he, not some giddy society Miss.

Then, Hugh meets Helena and despite their resolve, fate, it seems, has other ideas. As their attraction deepens however, treachery threatens to tear them apart. Will they uncover the perpetrator in time, or will their love be swept away, lost forever on a winter's tide?

A Love Unquenchable

Linen and Lace - Book Four

Jessica Drummond, a bright and cheerful young woman, rarely gives romance, let alone love, a thought. Long hours working in her brother's shipping office affords little chance of her ever meeting an eligible bachelor.

Duncan Barrington, veteran of the Napoleonic Wars, believes himself wounded in both body and soul. He has no intention of inflicting his demons on anyone, certainly not a beautiful and, in his opinion, irresponsible city lady.

One cold and snowy morning, the plight of a bedraggled puppy throws Jessica and Duncan together and, as a spark of something indefinable yet wholly unquenchable begins to burn, it is unclear who rescued whom.

A Hidden Rose

Linen and Lace - Book Five

After witnessing his mother's grief at the loss of his father, Nick

Drummond resolved never to cause someone he loved such distress. Even the happiness of his siblings would not sway him – until he met Rose.

Rose Archer was almost content assisting her doctor father in a tiny fishing village in the north of Yorkshire. To experience the world beyond, a tantalising dream – until she met Nick.

Unexpectedly, the impossible becomes possible, and the renounced – desired above all things, but the shipwreck that brought them together, may yet tear them apart. Will Nick learn to trust his heart, or will his love for Rose remain forever hidden

The Daffodil Garden

Horrifically scarred during the war, William Harcourt - Marquis of Blackthorne - prefers to spend his days in the quiet of his daffodil garden; plants do not pity, turn away, or judge.

Lucy Truscott, whose life is far removed from that of the *ton*, has no idea that by saving the life of a young woman, to whom she bears an uncanny resemblance, her own will be placed in mortal danger.

A chance encounter leads to something more. William begins to trust that Lucy sees the man beneath the scars, while Lucy is persuaded that love might actually transcend status.

Unfortunately, before their courtship has really begun, someone has every intention of ending it - permanently.

The Unconventional Duchess

Refusing to suffer the humiliation of her husband flaunting his mistress at Society events, the newly married Duchess of Wallingstead, Ella Lennox, takes control of her life. She leaves London for the family's country seat in remote Yorkshire.

A woman alone, Ella spends the next four years turning a cold, grim house into a home, and transforming the fortunes of the estate. Not afraid of hard work, she soon earns the respect of those around her with her determination and unconventional attitude.

Out of the blue, the duke arrives. Resigned to another arduous visit, Ella is stunned when it seems he is attempting to court her.

Impossible!

Could her dream of a happy marriage be about to come true?

Everything hangs on a snowstorm, a herd of cows and an uninvited guest!

Rescuing Her Knight

The de Wiltons - Book One

A story, invented to keep a little girl distracted, marks the beginning of another tale. One destined to remain unfinished for nearly twenty years.

Against her better judgement, Kitty de Wilton is persuaded to help Adam Marchmain banish his demons. This requires a subterfuge which, if discovered, might shatter more than the bonds of friendship forged two decades previously.

To Kitty, determined to break through the shield Adam has erected, the risk is worth it.

To see his smile and hear his laughter.

To rescue the knight of her childhood.

Just when a fairy tale ending is within her grasp, Kitty is threatened by the man who murdered her husband. In a cruel twist the tables are turned, and Kitty is the one who needs rescuing.

His Fiery Hoyden

A Novella

Livvy has no respect for the nobility; they let her down when she most needed them. Why should she accede to their demands now?

Philip, Lord Harrington, is stunned to discover the young heir to the dukedom lives a stone's throw away in a ramshackle cottage, and resolves to restore the child to his birthright.

They meet in a clash of wills, but just when it seems Livvy might surrender, the victory Philip desires, may not taste all that sweet.

A Regency Duet

Luck be a Pirate

Luck wasn't something retired pirate Kennet Alexson believed in – good or bad. However, even he had to concede that landing a job at Trentams shipyard, and meeting Lynette Collins, was more than coincidence.

Fortune it seemed, was smiling on him for once.

As Kennet adjusts to life on dry land, his friendship with Lynette deepens into something far more enduring, and what once seemed elusive now becomes possible.

Unfortunately, fate has other plans, and Kennet's good luck is about to run out.

The Highwayman's Kiss

Surrendered Hearts – Book One

Nothing exciting had ever happened to Juliette St Clair. Her days were spent assisting her father or calling on friends, wandering art galleries, taking constitutionals or, and more preferably, escaping into her books. Her evenings her evenings — an endless round of balls, where she preferred to remain invisible.

Until the day she was robbed by a highwayman.

A Regency Christmas Double

Heart Rescued

Four years since Jasper lost the woman he was hoping to marry. Four years since he closed his heart and withdrew from Society. He has no idea his reclusive existence is about to be shattered.

Enter his sister's best friend, Harriet, a flame haired beauty, who needs his help.

Reluctantly he agrees and as they spend time together, it is clear their feelings run deep. Although Harriet affects Jasper in a way no woman ever has, he believes her to be out of his league ~ but it's Christmas and she might just be the one to melt his frozen heart

Catch a Snowflake

Romance often blossoms in the most unlikely of places - but in a ward full of wounded soldiers - surely not?

When Lucas Withers comes face to face with Jemima Parsons - a young woman who blames him for her brother's injury - falling in love is the last thing on their minds. What neither of them anticipated, was the magic of snowflakes.

Fate is Curious

A Novella

Happily, ever after? No such thing! Bereft, following her beloved husband's sudden death, Lady Charlotte Sherbrooke has lost her belief in such romantic nonsense.

Successful shipping merchant, Zacharie Romain, is no stranger to loss; his business can be hazardous. Moreover, his wife died in childbirth and even though it happened a decade ago, he has no mind to expose himself to such sorrow again.

They meet in less than joyful circumstances but, as the year turns and grief diminishes, the woes of a small boy become the catalyst for something wholly unexpected. Can Charlotte and Zacharie trust what Fate has in store or will past heartbreak prevent them from taking a chance on love?

A Christmas Prayer

with Ashlee Shades

A Short Story

An entreaty from a frightened child.

Orphaned and only nine, Caroline Thorne has to grow up before her time. She is doing everything she can to keep what is left of her family together and out of the workhouse but is terrified her prayers are not being heard. Or maybe they are…

A petition from a woman desperate for a family.

A chance meeting with three orphaned siblings, tugs at Elizabeth Barrington's heart strings. Thus far, she and her husband have not been blessed with children and, as Christmas approaches, a plan begins to form - one which might just be the answer to her prayers.

Two Christmas prayers, as different as they are the same.

Will they hear and, more importantly, heed the answer?

The Lady's Wager

Surrendered Hearts- Book Two

A Novelette

Ged Mowbray will do anything to avoid being married off to the suitable prospects his parents insist on parading in front of him.

Melissa Bouchard is under no illusion her sizeable dowry is the attraction to suitors, not her.

An overheard conversation leads to an offer too good to refuse, but what happens when a lady's wager, becomes a gamble on the happily ever after, you did not even realise you wanted?

Winning Emma

Surrendered Hearts - Book Three

A Novelette

Randolph Craythorpe — earl, covert operative, and occasional highwayman — believed his dalliance with Lady Felicity Hartwich would lead to marriage. It did, but not to him! The arrival of an unwelcome guest, however, provides the perfect opportunity to indulge in a little retaliation.

Emma Newbury accompanies her cousin, Lady Charity Anscombe, to London for the Christmas season. Once there, she comes face to face with the three men who witnessed the humiliating aftermath of her father's disgrace — one of whom, to her irritation, has taken up residence in her dreams.

Their infrequent encounters only serve to confuse but, while winter tightens its grip on the city, what was inconceivable becomes the one thing for which they both yearn, yet bound by Society's rules, cannot admit.

As the snow falls, Randolph begins to understand that to win Emma, he will have to surrender.

A Love Impossible

A Regency M/M Novelette

Tasked with investigating a heinous crime, Edward Lindsay travels from London to Dublin — a city which holds too many memories — in the guise of guardian to his sister. He knew it could be hazardous, and relished the challenge, but that wasn't what caused his stomach to tighten as they approached landfall.

Dublin held more than just a murderer.

There was also Aidan.

While attending a party, Aidan Griffen is astonished when he comes face to face with a man who fled Dublin two years previously. A man he has desperately tried to forget.

As Edward closes in on his quarry, a fire, deliberately extinguished, is rekindled. But what of it? Edward and Aidan share a love impossible, and to acknowledge their feelings — more dangerous than confronting a killer.

Is there any hope of a happily ever after?

Unravelling Roana

A Novelette

Tired of being ignored by her husband, Roana Dumont, Countess of Brooketon does the one thing guaranteed to get his attention. She runs away... to Venice, leaving behind a set of riddles for him to solve... *if* he feels their marriage is worth saving.

Gideon Dumont, 6th Earl of Brooketon is flabbergasted when he discovers his wife has apparently vanished off the face of the earth. A series of puzzles, the only clue as to her whereabouts.

The question is... will he unravel them?

FAIRY TALE ROMANCE

Chasing Bluebells

A Novella

Once upon a time, somewhere in France, there was a man whose reckless obsession led him down a dark path. One which, ultimately, cost him his life.

That ought to have been the end of it. Regrettably, as is so often the case, those who least deserve it, suffer for the actions of others.

A decade after being sent away, Sebastien Daviau returns to the little village where everything began, hoping to lay the ghosts of his childhood to rest, studiously ignoring the possibility, he might run into Charlotte de Montbeliard.

As luck would have it, Charlotte is the one who runs into him… well his horse. Although the encounter leaves a lasting impression, neither recognises the other.

A name revealed causes a freak accident, catapulting Sebastien's past into his present, and bringing him face to face with a man whose reputation would intimidate the most ardent of suitors.

Can whatever is blossoming between Charlotte and Sebastien survive the challenge imposed, or is their happily ever after about to fade as quickly as the bluebells they loved to chase?

CONTEMPORARY ROMANCES

Of Ruins and Romance

While escorting a group of tourists around the ancient Roman port of Ostia, Kassandra Winters bumps into someone she first met in less than auspicious circumstances two years previously. The encounter leads to a job offer - to be the assistant guide for a three-week tour of ancient sites in and around Rome. Unable to resist such an opportunity, Kassie agrees.

Kassie has intrigued Gabriel St Germain since he accidentally knocked her flying outside her university professor's office. Her face haunts his dreams, yet he never expected to see her again. So, he is surprised when she appears, as though destined to do so, in the middle of a ruin, and he concocts a plan to win her heart.

Gabriel's old-fashioned courtship touches something deep inside Kassie and, although struggling to believe someone as handsome as Gabriel could possibly be interested in her, she soon realises she has fallen irrevocably in love with him. However, just as Kassie shares everything of herself with Gabriel, her world comes crashing down. Can their romance survive, or will it fall in ruins, like the relics of antiquity that brought them together?

All At Once It's You

When Alex arrives in the small village of Rosedale Abbey, to take up a position as a research assistant for a renowned archaeologist, the last thing she is looking for, or expects to find, is love.

Jake was perfectly happy with the status quo. When it came to relationships, he didn't do committed or long term. He called the shots, and if his current flame didn't like it, she knew what to do. A philosophy, which served him well - until he met Alex.

Romance blooms, but even as the untamed wilderness of the North Yorkshire moors weaves its spell, a long-buried secret might yet jeopardise their happily ever after.

Cobweb Dreams

A Contemporary Novella

A holiday on the Scottish isle of Mull was just the break Chloe Shepherd needed, an escape from her boring office job and her complete lack of anything resembling a social life. Romance, it seems, isn't on the cards and, although Chloe dreams of finding her soulmate she is beginning to believe love is like cobwebs — spun overnight, only to vanish in the early morning breeze.

Under sufferance, Dominic Winters makes a flying visit to Mull to check on a rental property owned by his family. He hasn't got time for this — so indulging in a holiday fling is the last thing on his mind.

A lamb stuck in a bog proves a most unexpected matchmaker and, while Mull weaves its magic, Chloe wonders whether those fragile cobwebs might be far more stubborn than she thought.

Just One Step

A Short Story

In the aftermath of an horrific car accident, Daisy Forrester travels to Italy - hoping, so far from her memories, she might begin to heal.

Archaeologist, and single father, Adam Willoughby is too busy looking after his young daughter to give romance let alone love, a thought.

Neither expects a chance encounter in an ancient ruin to be anything more, but sometimes, that's all it takes.

His Heart's Second Sigh

A Novella

Reuben Faulkner and Paige Latimer are two happily single people, who have no desire to upset the status quo.

Unexpectedly, they are thrown together, only to discover both want far more than a casual friendship.

Just when things take an interesting turn, Reuben's past catches up with them, and threatens to derail their blossoming romance before it has chance to start.